Dinosaurs
Living in
MY HAIR!

by Jayne M. Rose-Vallee
illustrated by Anni Matsick

Jayne M. Rose-Vallee
2014

Dinosaurs Living in MY HAIR!

First Edition 2015
ISBN 978-0-9861922-0-3

Visit our web site to find available dinosaur products
rosevalleecreations.com
or visit us on Facebook
facebook.com/dinosaursinmyhair

Please look for new *Dinosaurs Living in My Hair!* adventures coming soon.

FSC Certified Recycled Paper
Made in USA

ROSEVALLEE
CREATIONS

To Lauren Danielle, the real life Sabrina, who inspires,
motivates and empowers others to reach their dreams.
I dedicate this book to you with love and admiration.
"I love you this much!"

My Name is Sabrina
And I look like this.
At my birthday next week
I'm going to be SIX!

My curls are a challenge
To live with each day.
"Creatures could hide out there,"
My mom likes to say.

Underneath all this mess,
Tangled up in my hair,
What if there are dinosaurs
Living in there?

Dinosaurs

Living

In

My

Hair

?? !! ?? !!

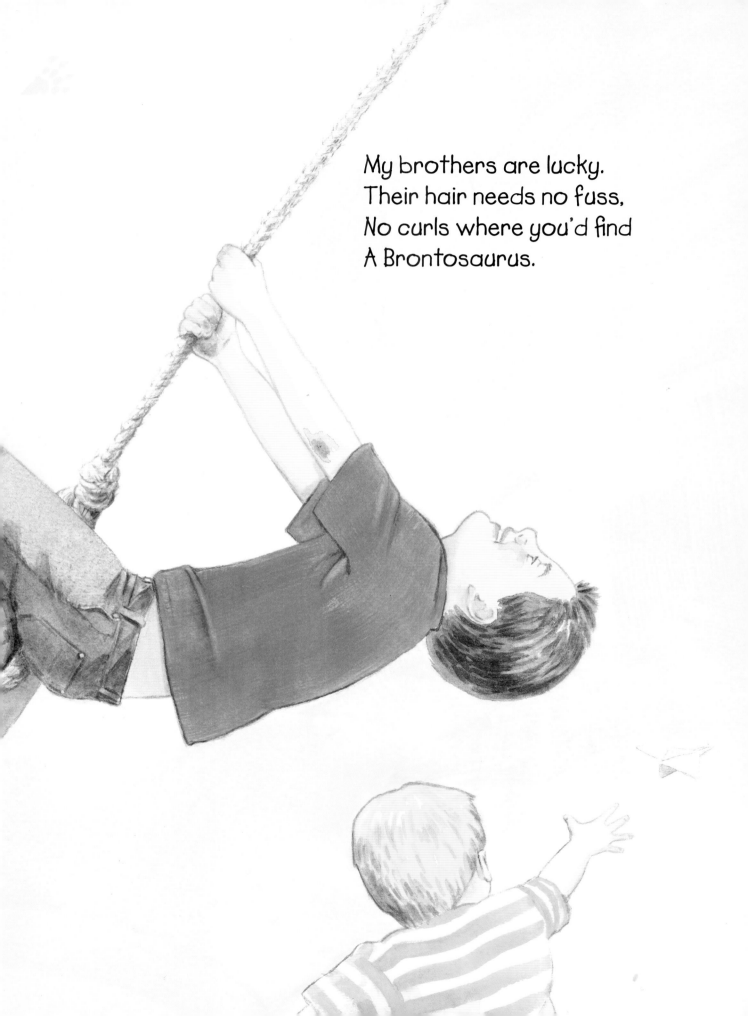

My brothers are lucky.
Their hair needs no fuss,
No curls where you'd find
A Brontosaurus.

Each day when I wake,
I climb out of bed.
I peek in my mirror
To inspect my curled head.

I lift each curl slowly
And peer underneath,
Hopeful nothing stares back
With snarling sharp teeth.

It's been millions of years
Since dinosaurs roamed.
Could they possibly live
Beneath where I comb?

I wish it weren't me.
I wish it were Mom.
I must remain quiet,
Unruffled and calm.

The clock chimes eight-thirty.
My mom yells, "Get Dressed!"
A few minutes later
She calls up, "Breakfast."

My brothers are noisy.
Their room's next to mine.
They're ready in seconds.
It takes them NO time.

Dressing lickety-split,
I am ready to go.
As I walk from my bedroom,
I grab my pink bow.

I run to the bathroom
To find my blue comb.
I know it won't help much.
I let out a groan.

The combing and brushing
Does little to help,
Still plenty of places
To hide at my scalp.

I think I see movement.
Is Mom really right?
Do dinosaurs live
In my hair out of sight?

Do they live in my curls,
I reason and factor.
Are those eyes looking back
Attached to a raptor?

I try not to panic.
I brush my teeth next.
But what if I'm wrong and
It was a T-Rex?

I enter the kitchen
And Mom looks relieved.
Her eyes spot my hairdo.
She doesn't look pleased.

My mom says, "Oh dear,
Let me help you with that."
As she brushes my hair,
Out flies a black bat.

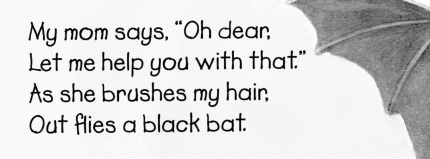

I tell her, "That's nothing
To worry about —
The problem is getting
Those dinosaurs out."

The tangles are many.
She combs through again.
I scrunch up my face.

WHEN

WILL

THIS

ALL

END?

With my bow in my hair
And my curls all in place,
My mother insists,
"What a beautiful face!"

"The creatures have vanished
I brushed them all out."
I give Mom a hug,
But I still have my doubts.

My brothers are yelling,
"Let's go, Time for school!"
I grab my new backpack
Adorned with pink jewels.

As I walk out the door,
I glance in the mirror.
My eyes quickly widen.
I'm filled with great fear.

As I'm walking to school,
I know I'm afraid.
I keep asking myself,

"What

if

Dinos

lay

eggs?"

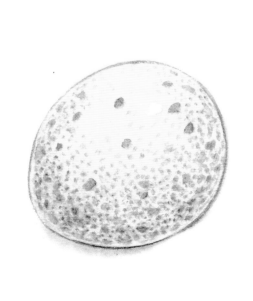